D1459841

CONTENTS

Acknowledgments:
The photograph on page 48 is by courtesy of BBC Hulton Picture Library, and that on page 36 by courtesy of D. Constance Ltd; the picture on page 5 is reproduced by courtesy of the Trustees, The National Gallery, London; that on page 12 by courtesy of the Trustees, The National Portrait Gallery, London; and that on page 32 (bottom) by courtesy of the Mansell Collection.

Published by Ladybird Books Ltd Loughborough Leicestershire UK
Ladybird Books Inc Auburn Maine 04210 USA
Printed in England (3)

Book 2

Kings and Queens

written by BRENDA RALPH LEWIS
illustrated by JOHN LEIGH-PEMBERTON,
PETER ROBINSON and FRANK HUMPHRIS

Ladybird Books

Longleat House, a typical example of Renaissance architecture

Introduction

When King Henry VII won his crown in battle at Bosworth Field in 1485, the world outside England was changing in many exciting ways. The *Renaissance* (rebirth) of the Ancient Greek and Roman civilisations brought with it new ideas of art, architecture, astronomy, science and medicine. Venturesome seamen, chiefly the Portuguese, were exploring the oceans outside Europe for the first time. Except in very remote areas, it was becoming less and less necessary for people to live in castles or walled towns.

Europe, in other words, was settling down and becoming more civilised after the long, dangerous centuries of the Middle Ages.

The invention of firearms was sweeping away the age of the heavily-armoured knight, the mainstay of the private armies kept by medieval barons. The feudal system, which made

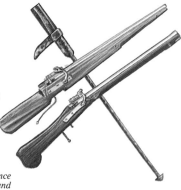

Early firearms of the Renaissance period. A 16th century hackbut and two 16th century matchlocks

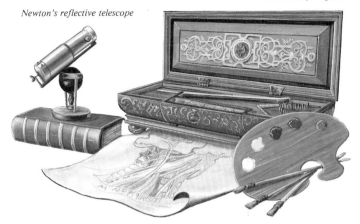

the barons so powerful, had largely disappeared, and the power of the Pope in Rome to order and control the affairs of European countries was not nearly as great as before.

Now, the king was becoming the greatest, most powerful and most important person in the land – and that was something which particularly suited Henry VII.

During the Wars of the Roses, the crown of England had been virtually a plaything for the nobles to squabble over, and kings and princes had been killed and murdered in the brutal struggle for power. In these circumstances, Henry VII had to restore honour and respect, not only to the crown of England, but to the man who wore it.

Madonna and Child with St Anne
by Leonardo da Vinci, a Renaissance artist
(The National Gallery, London)

THE TUDORS
King Henry VII – 1485-1509

Henry reacted by having Yorkist claimants hunted down and killed, exiled or executed. Other troublemakers were treated just as harshly. Disobedient nobles were kept in order with heavy taxes, fines or confiscations of their land. Wisely, King Henry kept nobles out of positions of power by choosing humble commoners as advisers: that way, advisers had no authority except the authority given them by the king. Previous kings, who had to ask Parliament for money, had been at Parliament's mercy. Henry VII provided

Of the seven kings of England before Henry VII, only one, Henry V, succeeded peacefully to the throne and died in his bed. Would Henry VII be any luckier? To the end of his reign, Henry was never absolutely certain, for his Yorkist rivals for the crown hatched one plot after another to unseat him. This included trying to pass off two impostors: Lambert Simnel in 1487 and Perkin Warbeck in 1497, as 'rightful heirs' to the throne.

Early Tudor costume was much more dignified than in previous reigns. Beautiful materials were imported from Italy and the East, such as Damask, a rich silk from Damascus

Initials and trademark of Caxton, the first British printer.
The Age of Learning was helped by the invention of movable metal type which made printed material more widely available

himself with his own income, by taxing imported goods or making new tenants on royal estates pay large amounts before they could receive their lands.

Once, kings of England had been seen as mighty warriors or great lawgivers or both. Now, the king was a businessman, arranging trading treaties with foreign countries and staying up late at night to check the royal accounts. It was not glamorous or glorious, but this was how Henry VII made royal power strong and respected once more. For he knew, and his subjects knew, that if this were not so, the bloodshed and anarchy of the Wars of the Roses could start all over again.

In 1497, John Cabot discovered North America, four years after Columbus. Henry awarded him £10 and an annual pension of £20

7

King Henry VIII – 1509-1547

When the miserly Henry VII was succeeded by his 18-year old son, Henry VIII, the new king seemed to be a true king of the new Renaissance Age – young, handsome, charming and well educated enough to discuss scholarly subjects with learned men. However, beneath this brilliant exterior there lay a cruel despot.

That became clear after 1529 when Henry began trying to divorce his first wife, Catherine of Aragon, who had failed to give him the son he so desperately wanted. Henry wanted to marry Catherine's lady-in-waiting, Anne Boleyn. However, the Pope in Rome refused Henry his divorce, and even the clever Cardinal Wolsey, who had run England for Henry for twenty years, could not get the Pope to change his mind. Wolsey was charged with treason, and only his death in 1530 saved him from being put on trial. Then Henry began illtreating Catherine and their daughter Mary, to force Catherine to agree that her marriage was illegal. Catherine refused. Finally, Henry made himself

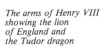

The arms of Henry VIII showing the lion of England and the Tudor dragon

head of the English Church, in place of the Pope, and pronounced his own divorce. Later, with the help of another clever minister, Thomas Cromwell, Henry closed the monasteries in England (1536-1539) and took their wealth. The monks and nuns were thrown out, and many had to beg for a living.

Henry was now a feared and fearsome ruler: to incur his displeasure often meant death. That was the fate of Thomas Cromwell, two of his six wives, including Anne Boleyn, and almost all the surviving Plantagenets, the previous royal family.

Little wonder that before Henry died in 1547, he was regarded with terror and dread.

THE SIX WIVES OF HENRY

Catherine of Aragon

Anne Boleyn

Jane Seymour

Anne of Cleves

Catherine Howard

Catherine Parr

King Edward VI – 1547-1553

Edward VI, son of Henry VIII's third wife, Jane Seymour, was only nine when he came to the throne. This was a dangerous situation, for it meant that ambitious men close to the king had the chance to take his power and use it for their own ends. So it soon proved. First, the young king's uncle, Edward Seymour, Duke of Somerset, overthrew the Regency Council Henry VIII had set up for his son, and made himself Protector. In 1551, however, Somerset was overthrown by the ruthless John Dudley, Duke of Northumberland. Somerset and Northumberland both ruled like despots, though Northumberland was much more ruthless. He used brute force to impose new Protestant church services on the people. When they rebelled, Northumberland suppressed them with yet

The Lord Protector arguing in front of the boy king at a Council of State

Peasants being forced off the land by the new land enclosures

more force. He used the same method to end unrest when the peasants protested over the enclosure of land, which robbed them of fields to grow their food and graze their cattle.

Then suddenly, Northumberland's power was put in danger when King Edward became dangerously ill in 1552. Mary, daughter of Catherine of Aragon, was Edward's heir and a devout Catholic. So, to cheat Mary of the throne and to stop her bringing Catholicism back to England, Northumberland hatched a plot. He arranged a marriage between his son and Edward's second cousin, Lady Jane Grey. Then he forced the dying young king to disinherit Mary and name Lady Jane as his successor. On 6th July 1553, after dreadful suffering, 15-year old King Edward died. But immediately, Northumberland found that his plot had gone seriously wrong.

The Church of England Prayer Book printed in English during Edward VI's reign

Queen Mary I – 1553-1558

(National Portrait Gallery, London)

In July 1553, Edward VI's half-sister, Mary, became queen of England amid great popular rejoicing. The people absolutely refused to accept Lady Jane Grey, the 'queen' Northumberland had tried to impose on them, and wholeheartedly greeted Mary as the true heir to the throne. Northumberland was later executed for treason.

Yet only five years later, Queen Mary died, loathed and detested by her people. For many years 17th November, the date of her death in 1558, and therefore Elizabeth I's accession was kept as a public holiday.

What went wrong? The answer lies with Mary herself, for she became a queen who was ruthlessly determined to wreak revenge on her Protestant enemies, and to restore Catholicism in England. Landowners who had bought former Church lands were infuriated when Mary demanded that they give them up and restore them to the Church. Protestants were enraged when Mary made the English church loyal again to the Pope in Rome. Almost everyone objected fiercely when, in 1554, Mary married the Catholic Prince Philip of Spain, and allowed Spaniards

King Philip II of Spain

Burning Protestant heretics

virtually to control the government. Finally, Mary sickened her subjects by ordering the burning of some 300 Protestant 'heretics' – most of them ordinary Englishmen and women.

By the time she died, Queen Mary had failed in every possible way. Philip, whom she loved dearly, did not return her love: he had married Mary only to strengthen the alliance between England and Spain. Her subjects hated Catholicism more than ever before, and even before her death they were calling her by a name that persists to this day: 'Bloody Mary'.

16th century pendant housed in the Royal collection at Windsor

Queen Elizabeth I – 1558-1603

The Elizabethan era was one of poetry, art, music and great architecture

When Elizabeth I, daughter of Henry VIII and Anne Boleyn, succeeded Mary as queen in 1558, she possessed two great advantages. Firstly, Elizabeth was a Protestant. Secondly, she was 'all English', unlike Mary whose mother had been Spanish.

In addition, however, Elizabeth had the qualities of a powerful and popular monarch, for she had a natural talent for wise, moderate government. Elizabeth chose as her advisers men of great ability: Sir William Cecil, better known as Lord Burghley, who served her until his death in 1598, and his son Robert. Between them, Elizabeth and the Cecils handled Parliament carefully and tactfully and Parliament was now very strong and influential. Elizabeth was, by nature, rather despotic.

However, she knew she had to win Parliament's co-operation, particularly in the tricky business of making a religious settlement after so many years of violence and upheaval.

Elizabeth succeeded, for under the Acts of Supremacy and Uniformity (1559), she made possible the gradual spread of the new Protestant religion, without offending the Catholics too much: for instance, the 1552 Protestant Prayer Book was altered to make it easier for Catholics to accept.

Elizabeth wisely realised that her subjects loathed the idea of foreign influence in England – particularly after the Spaniards had controlled the government during Mary's reign. This was one reason why Elizabeth never married, although she had many suitors, including Philip of Spain, Mary's former husband.

Performance of one of Shakespeare's plays. All the women's parts were played by young men

Instead, Queen Elizabeth preferred to be 'married' to her country and her people. Elizabeth's court became a centre of culture for English musicians, poets, scholars and artists, like William Byrd, the composer, Nicholas Hilliard, the painter and Sir Walter Raleigh, the poet and adventurer. This was also the age of great English writers, like the dramatists, William Shakespeare and Christopher Marlowe.

Mary Queen of Scots was the mother of Elizabeth's successor, James I. She was imprisoned for nineteen years before her execution in 1587

Elizabeth herself had great charm, intelligence and pride in being English. Although she was rather vain and quick tempered, she had a great talent for inspiring loyalty. She also had considerable courage, and when England seemed in grave danger from Spanish invasion in 1588, Elizabeth went down personally to Tilbury to speak to the crews of the ships that were going to do battle with the great Spanish Armada. "I know I am a weak and feeble woman," Elizabeth told her sailors, "but I have the heart and stomach of a king – and a King of England, too!"

This was marvellously stirring stuff, and afterwards, when the English fleet won a great victory against the Armada, Elizabeth's subjects felt great pride in their country, their navy – and their queen.

Victory over the Spanish Armada

This was a time, too, when England was becoming more important in the world, and English sailors were challenging the Spaniards in the new, rich Spanish colonies in America. Seamen like the famous Francis Drake, John Hawkins or Martin Frobisher made daring raids on the Spaniards and captured their treasure ships. Drake became the first Englishman to sail round the world (1577-1580) and John Hawkins designed and built ships in Devon shipyards which were the best and fastest galleons

Sir Walter Raleigh introduced potatoes and tobacco into this country

in the world.

Queen Elizabeth seemed to personify this age of daring adventure, and as a result, she was given names like 'the Sun Queen' or 'Gloriana'.

Francis Drake is knighted on board the Golden Hind

THE STUARTS
King James I – 1603-1625

After the inspiring Elizabeth, her successor, James I, was something of a shock. He had no kingly dignity with his large bulging eyes, spindly legs and slovenly appearance. Furthermore, James was a foreigner – he was already James VI of Scotland and inherited the English throne because he was descended from Margaret, elder daughter of Henry VII. James was also tactless, and soon deeply angered his English subjects by persecuting both the Catholics and the extreme Protestant Puritans. The Catholics responded with many plots against James: one was the famous Gunpowder Plot to blow up Parliament in 1605. To escape from James, one group of persecuted Protestants – the

Arresting one of the conspirators of the Gunpowder Plot

The Pilgrim Fathers set sail for America in the Mayflower

'Pilgrim Fathers' – sailed to America in 1620.

James believed in the 'Divine Right of Kings' – the idea that kings were appointed by God and could rule as they pleased – so inevitably, he quarrelled with Parliament. When Parliament objected to James' favourites and his extravagance, James reacted by ruling without Parliament (1614-1621). He obtained money by forcing loans from landowners or selling official posts.

In 1621 Parliament hit back and accused James' Chancellor of corruption, and his Treasurer of treason. Both were deprived of their positions and forbidden to hold government posts again. Then, in 1624, James failed in his very unpopular plan to marry his son, Charles, to a Spanish Catholic princess. Parliament had been outraged at the idea – and now, James was getting old and tired. At last, he gave in and agreed to let Parliament share in government. However, in 1625, James died and Parliament soon discovered that his successor, Charles, was an even more stubborn opponent.

King Charles I – 1625-1649

On 20th January 1649, King Charles I became the only king of England to be put on trial by his subjects, and ten days later, the only one to be publicly executed. Charles was NOT the first, however, to make the mistakes which brought him to this terrible end.

Charles believed in the 'Divine Right of Kings', and put his trust in unpopular favourites who meddled in government affairs. When Parliament criticised Charles' government, Charles dismissed them and ruled alone (1629-1640). He raised money by imposing his own taxes, some of them illegal.

None of this was new – Parliament had been through it all before with James I. However, now Parliament was dominated by Puritans who wanted to strip Charles of his royal powers. Charles, for his part, was extremely stubborn, the sort who would never give in. He decided to teach these upstart Puritans a lesson, and went with an armed guard to the House of Commons to arrest five of them in 1642. The five, however, had been warned and were in hiding.

King and Parliament were now totally opposed to one another. There was only one

The Stuart coat of arms.
The unicorn has replaced the Tudor dragon. (Compare this with the picture on page 8)

possible outcome – civil war. At first, it seemed as if Charles was going to win, particularly after the first big battle, at Edgehill in 1642. Parliament, however, soon acquired a new, highly disciplined army – the 'New Model' Army, or 'Ironsides' trained by Oliver Cromwell. Charles' royalists were thrashed at Marston Moor in 1644 and at Naseby in 1645.

In 1646, Charles gave himself up to the Scots but they handed him over to the English. Charles escaped in 1647, but was again captured in 1648 and put on trial in 1649 in Westminster Hall for making war on his own subjects. Charles refused to answer the charge, claiming the court had no right to try him. By 68 votes to 67, the court sentenced Charles to death.

Cavaliers (Royalists) and Roundheads during the Civil War

Oliver Cromwell – 1653-1658

Costumes of about 1640 were very elaborate with lace collars, ribbons and ruffs. During Cromwell's time Puritan clothes became drab, dull and without ornament

After Charles' execution, Parliament abolished the monarchy and declared England a republic. Real power, however, lay with the Army and with Oliver Cromwell, who became Lord Protector in 1653. Soon, strangely, history began repeating itself, for Cromwell quarrelled with Parliament. Parliament refused Cromwell money and it had criticised his government. Cromwell responded, like Charles, by dismissing Parliament and ruling without it.

Under Cromwell's rule, the army and the navy became very powerful and at sea English ships won tremendous victories over the Dutch. At home, however, England was becoming a gloomy, joyless place. Theatres and public houses were closed, for Puritans thought they were sinful. People were fined for playing games or travelling on Sundays, and colourful dress and merrymaking were very much frowned on.

Before long, the English grew tired of Puritanism and republicanism, and longed for a king again.

17th century coach

Many stained glass windows were smashed in Puritan times

In 1658, Cromwell died. His son and successor, Richard, could not control the Army and Parliament, who were at loggerheads, and it seemed that England would sink into chaos. There was only one thing to do. Prince Charles, exiled son and heir of the dead king, had to be invited back.

King Charles II – 1660-1685

On 29th May 1660, his thirtieth birthday, King Charles II entered London to a great welcome. Everyone seemed happy that England was a monarchy again, especially as Charles had promised everyone the freedom to follow their own religion, and brought with him a return to the jollity the gloomy Puritans had suppressed. Parliament was content because Charles was willing to ask for, and heed, its advice on government.

But things did not work out so happily. Many royalists wanted to take revenge on the Puritans, and both they and the Catholics were cruelly persecuted. Charles, for his part, was not always the lighthearted 'Merry Monarch', of his nickname. Charles had suffered bitter years in exile, and was determined, as he put it, "not to go on my travels again". Charles therefore kept hidden two beliefs he knew were very unpopular: his belief in the 'Divine Right of Kings' and his attraction to Roman Catholicism. However, Parliament was terrified of another civil war, and another military dictator like Oliver Cromwell. So Charles II was able to act despotically at times without Parliament punishing him as it had punished his father.

King Charles takes a stroll

24

Narrow, dirty streets which encouraged the spread of the Plague of London in 1665

Like his father, Charles ruled without Parliament from time to time. What was more, he ensured that his royalist supporters held positions of power as magistrates in county courts or as town councillors. Charles even managed to resist attempts to deprive his brother, James, of his right to succeed him as king. This was no easy task, for James was a fanatical Catholic and, unlike Charles, made no secret of his faith.

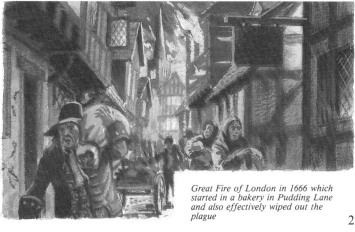

Great Fire of London in 1666 which started in a bakery in Pudding Lane and also effectively wiped out the plague

King James II – 1685-1688

When King James II came to the throne in 1685, his aims were the most dangerous ones possible. He intended to make England a Catholic country again, and to rule according to the 'Divine Right of Kings', with total power. James announced he would ignore any laws he did not like, and when Parliament protested, he dismissed Parliament.

James then proceeded to put Catholics in positions of power: one became, for instance, Lord Lieutenant of Ireland. When James cancelled the laws against Catholics, the Archbishop of Canterbury and six bishops protested. James had them arrested and put on trial.

Needless to say, James was exceedingly unpopular with his furious subjects, but no one wanted to take up arms against the king in another civil war. So, since James' Protestant daughter, Princess Mary, would one day succeed him, the English decided to put up with their outrageous king.

The Archbishop of Canterbury is arrested

William lands in England at Torbay, with his army

Then, in 1688, everything changed. James' second wife, the Catholic Mary of Modena, gave birth to a son – and that meant a long line of Catholic monarchs.

To prevent it, important Protestants, including the former Bishop of London, secretly invited Princess Mary's husband, William, Prince of Orange (Holland) to come to England and save the country from the Catholic threat.

William came with an army in November 1688, and James soon found to his dismay that his own troops were deserting him and joining the invaders. James became afraid he would have his head chopped off, like his father, and fled to France.

For a few weeks after this, there was no king on the throne. This is called an *inter-regnum*.

The successors of King James II
King William III – 1689-1702
Queen Mary II – 1689-1694
Queen Anne – 1702-1714

During the reign of William and Mary, men wore 'arched' wigs. It was fashionable for women to be plump

Protestant England could not have had a better champion than Prince William of Orange, for he was the great warrior-protector of Protestantism in Europe. William was also a Stuart; a nephew of Charles II. An agreement was made whereby William and his wife, Mary, became joint King and Queen, with Mary's sister, Anne, as heir.

But first Parliament decided to place controls on royal power, and so do away with the 'Divine Right of Kings'.

Now, Parliament regulated the monarch's expenditure and kings had to ask Parliament's permission before employing an army in peacetime, or dismissing judges. A new Parliament would be called every three years, and under the Act of Settlement (1701) all future monarchs had to belong to the Church of England. In other words, no Catholic could occupy the throne and England's kings and queens became 'constitutional' monarchs, acting as advisers to, and partners with, Parliament.

The first constitutional monarchs of England were crowned as King William III and Queen Mary II in 1689. Mary was a good-tempered, unambitious woman, quite content to let William deal with Parliament and affairs of government. Although the marriage had been a political one, William was extremely fond of his wife, and was grief-stricken when she died of smallpox in 1694.

By that time, William had been accepted as king in Scotland, although not without bloodshed.

James II failed in his attempt to retrieve the throne at the Battle of Boyne in 1690

Macdonald of Glencoe, one of the Highland chieftains formerly opposed to William, had agreed, with the others, to take an oath of allegiance to him. Unfortunately, Glencoe was late in doing so, and a massacre of his clan followed in 1692.

This dreadful event helped to strengthen the Jacobites, the supporters of James, the son of James II, whose birth in 1688 had led to the 'Bloodless' Revolution. Nevertheless, when William died in 1702, Anne became Queen without opposition.

A passenger barge used along the Thames at the end of the 17th century

Queen Anne

The reign of Queen Anne, which lasted until 1714, was full of brilliant men, like Sir Christopher Wren, architect of St Paul's Cathedral, Sir Isaac Newton, the scientific genius and John Churchill, Duke of Marlborough, who was one of England's great military heroes.

Queen Anne herself was a somewhat dull woman, whose chief pleasures were playing cards and drinking tea. Anne felt very guilty about deserting her father, James II, but she was glad that the Anglican Church, to which she was devoted, had triumphed. Anne used some of her yearly income of

St Paul's Cathedral, designed by Christopher Wren

£50,000 from Parliament to establish 'Queen Anne's Bounty' for the benefit of poor clergymen.

Tragically, by 1700 all seventeen of Anne's children had died and it seemed there might be a dispute about her successor since the Catholic descendants of Charles I were still alive. So Parliament chose as Anne's heir the Protestant Sophia, Electress of Hanover and a grand-daughter of James I.

Sophia died in 1714, eight weeks before Queen Anne, and the new monarch, who landed at Greenwich on a foggy September day that year, was Sophia's son, and England's first Hanoverian king: George I.

John Churchill, First Duke of Marlborough and ancestor of Sir Winston Churchill, England's great leader during the Second World War

George I lands in Greenwich

31

The Five Hanoverian Kings – 1714-1837

The reigns of the five kings of the House of Hanover spanned some of the most important years in the history of Britain and Europe. Britain became a great industrial power with the advent of the Industrial Revolution (1750-1840).

After the end of the wars with the French emperor, Napoleon, in 1815, the British Navy was the most powerful in the world. Britain had a very rich trade and a growing overseas empire. Britain was also the most 'modern' and 'democratic' country, and the one most concerned with social reform.

These Hanoverian kings were not the most popular monarchs. In fact, they were an outrageous family and were often laughed at by cartoonists and writers. The Hanoverian kings and their families were undignified, and coarse in their manners. They had the horrible habit of spitting in public. The kings also quarrelled violently with their heirs, and exchanged dreadful insults.

32 Les Invisibles; *a satirical Hanoverian cartoon*

George I – 1714-1727

The Hanoverian kings were not accepted by everyone in Britain. In 1715, the year after George I became king, there was a Jacobite Rebellion which aimed to put James, the 'Old Pretender', son of King James II, on the throne. The Rebellion failed.

The first Hanoverian king had not been very pleased to become king of England. George I could not speak English, and never bothered to learn, which was why his place at meetings of government ministers was eventually taken over by a 'Chief' or 'Prime' Minister. Both George I and his son, George II, disliked being 'constitutional' monarchs and thought Parliament was a great nuisance. Both preferred their Electorate of Hanover, where they were 'absolute' rulers.

The Jacobite Rebellion

George II – 1727-1760

In 1745 the Scots invaded England for the last time. The invasion was led by 'Bonnie Prince Charlie' who, as grandson of James II, had a better claim to the throne than George. But Charles was beaten at Culloden and his cause lost for ever. It was said that George II was so frightened that he had his bags packed, ready to hurry back to Hanover. After the failure of this second rebellion the Highland Scots, who had supported it, were very cruelly punished.

During the reign of George II, the King had less and less influence in the Government.

Costume of the period.
Men's wigs were powdered and women wore mob caps and pannier skirts with hooped petticoats

Soldiers of the British Army. An officer of the King's Own Regiment of Foot (left) and a corporal of the Black Watch, which was founded in 1725 to prevent cattle stealing

34

George III – 1760-1820

King George III, the first English-born Hanoverian monarch and the first one who could speak English well, tried to bring back 'personal' royal rule in England after he came to the throne in 1760. He did this by using bribery to form his own political group, the 'King's Party', and through this ruled as a 'minister' in the government. This personal rule came to an end, however, after King George III and his minister, Lord North, tried to impose taxes on the American colonists without their consent. This was one of the chief causes of the American War of Independence, and after 1783, when the colonies won their freedom from Britain, George III's personal rule finally ended.

In France, in 1789, a revolution broke out and under Napoleon, France was victorious throughout Europe. Britain alone remained unconquered and finally Napoleon was beaten at sea, by Nelson, at the Battle of Trafalgar and on land, at Waterloo, by Wellington. George III reigned for 60 years, the second longest reign in British history.

The improvement in roads meant lighter, faster carriages such as this Phaeton of 1785

George IV – 1820-1830

When the Prince Regent, who had ruled for the mad George III since 1811, himself became king in 1820, his coronation was the most superb and spectacular occasion. The new king himself was described as looking like 'some georgeous bird of paradise'. But he was unpopular with the people because of his extravagances such as the building of Brighton Pavilion.

England was changing under the Georges. Steam engines were invented and factories built for spinning and weaving.

In 1825, Stephenson built the first railway and during George's father's reign, men like Telford and MacAdam had begun building good roads which made travelling much easier.

The courts of the Hanoverian kings were not very cultured, for they had none of the polish and elegance of their Stuart predecessors. Not until the Prince Regent and future George IV began to show a taste for beautiful clothes, fine furnishings and splendid houses did Hanoverians live grandly.

Royal Pavilion, Brighton

William IV – 1830-1837

George IV's successor, his brother William IV, was quite different. He disapproved of the splendid robes and the great banquets his brother had held, and even suggested that he could do without a coronation when he became king in 1830. This was strange, because William IV was absolutely thrilled to become king. On the first day of his reign, he was so excited that he jumped into his carriage and raced through the streets of London, grinning broadly at passers-by.

In 1832, the Great Reform Act was passed, giving the right to certain householders to vote in Parliamentary elections. In 1833, slavery was abolished in British territories. The longest reign in history began with William IV's death in 1837, when his 18 year old niece, Queen Victoria, came to the throne.

An early locomotive with train of open-topped carriages

Queen Victoria – 1837-1901

Queen Victoria and her husband, Prince Albert

Costume of Victorian England. 1855 saw the introduction of the crinoline. This was a petticoat supported by hoops of whalebone or steel

After the disreputable Hanoverian kings, it was high time the monarchy became more respectable. That was the opinion of Queen Victoria and her husband, Prince Albert of Saxe-Coburg-Gotha. Victoria and Albert lived a very respectable life with their family of four sons and five daughters, many of whom married into the royal families of Europe. Both Victoria and Albert strongly disapproved of immoral conduct. So much so that Albert became hysterical when he learned that his son, Edward, the heir to the throne, was having a

The Royal Albert Hall named in honour of Victoria's husband

love affair with an actress. Although Albert was never popular in England, and did not become Victoria's 'Prince Consort' until 1857, he had great influence on the queen. Victoria, for her part, adored her handsome husband, and when he died in 1861, she was overcome with grief. She shut herself away to mourn him and refused to appear in public for a long time. To the end of her long life, Victoria wore black in Albert's memory.

Victoria was very Hanoverian in many ways. She had Hanoverian stubbornness and hot temper and she was sometimes cruel and intolerant. Like the Hanoverian kings, she disliked her heir, and despite his protests refused to let him take part in government affairs. However, Victoria did possess a very strong sense of duty towards her subjects. As time went on, she acquired more and more subjects, for the British Empire grew to great size during her reign, and ultimately covered one quarter of the Earth's surface and one quarter of its population.

The Crystal Palace

Albert encouraged Victoria to become interested in the suffering of children working in the mines, the hard conditions in factories and the filthy living conditions which so many poor people had to endure. Albert believed, and Victoria agreed with him, that working class folk were far more worthy and loyal to the throne than the pleasure-loving, selfish aristocracy. Victoria saw herself as a kindly mother and her subjects as children who needed to be guided and protected, but not given too

Queen Victoria was loved by the people

much freedom. This was why Victoria disapproved of radical or liberal ideas, such as granting the right to vote to working class people and women.

Victoria was, of course, a constitutional monarch, but had strong political opinions and strong likes and dislikes when it came to the Prime Ministers who headed governments during her reign. Victoria hated William Gladstone, for instance: he was stuffy and pompous and much too liberal for Victoria's 'conservative' taste. On the other hand, Victoria adored Benjamin Disraeli, who was always paying her compliments. Disraeli made Victoria 'Empress of India' in 1877 and followed policies which increased British power in the world. When Disraeli died in 1881, Victoria was grief-stricken. However, when Gladstone died in 1898 she threw herself into a fearful rage because her sons helped to carry his coffin at the funeral.

By this time, Queen Victoria had reigned longer than any other English monarch, and in 1897 her Diamond Jubilee, commemorating the sixtieth anniversary of her accession to the throne, was celebrated with great festivity throughout the British Empire. Victoria was queen for almost four years more, dying at the age of 81 on 22nd January 1901.

Ladies dresses with bustles became a common sight in Victorian times and the bowler hat was introduced for men

King Edward VII – 1901-1910

Edward VII was nearly sixty when he became king in 1901. So his subjects already knew him well, and they loved him. It was easy to like the charming, witty Edward, who was so fond of enjoying himself at parties or the theatre or at horse race meetings. Whether as Prince or King, Edward was never aloof or haughty, but always concerned about the feelings of others and particularly about the sufferings of the poor.

King Edward had a great talent for dealing with people in a way that put them at their ease, and during his short reign, he made great personal efforts to increase friendship between nations. He became known, in fact, as 'Edward the Peacemaker'.

It was amazing that Edward should turn out to be so warm-hearted and likeable, for his childhood had been

Edward VII was the first king to own a motor car. The first Rolls Royce was built in 1907

wretched and frustrating. He was forced to study for long hours, with very little relaxation or leisure. Edward was not a natural scholar though, and his parents thought him stupid and lazy. They showed him no love or affection, because they did not think he deserved it. Because of all this, King Edward was determined that his own children should enjoy a happy family life. In this, Edward was extremely successful, and when he died in 1910, his son and successor, George V, wrote sorrowfully that he had lost 'the best of friends and the best of fathers'. Edward's subjects felt exactly the same way.

Edwardian dress

King Edward VII was keen on horse racing and three of his horses won the Derby

43

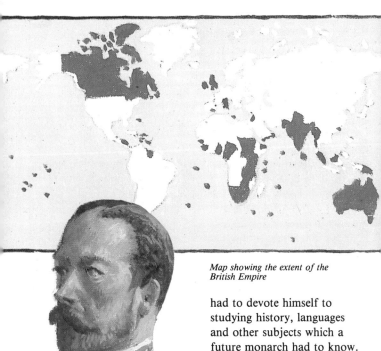

Map showing the extent of the British Empire

King George V – 1910-1936

King George V was very different from his father, Edward VII. George was quiet, serious-minded, rather shy and a bit stiff in his manner. By training, he was a naval officer and was later known as the 'Sailor King'. His naval career came to an end, though, when his elder brother died in 1892, and he had to devote himself to studying history, languages and other subjects which a future monarch had to know. Like Queen Victoria and Prince Albert, King George and his wife, Queen Mary, led a very respectable family life with their children, and devoted themselves wholeheartedly to their royal duties. These included many public duties, for now the royal family was expected to perform ceremonies like opening new bridges or public buildings, or visiting hospitals. Through this work, King George and Queen Mary became well known and much

Many thousands of lives were lost in the trenches during the First World War

respected public figures. Their popularity was a great asset at a time when one crisis seemed to follow another, and Britain was involved in the First World War (1914-1918) and the strikes, unemployment and unrest afterwards. Through all this, the British people seemed to know that in George V they had a conscientious king who cared greatly for his country. In 1935, when King George had been king for 25 years and celebrated his Silver Jubilee, his subjects showed tremendous enthusiasm for him. It was like a national birthday party. Sadly, though, the joy of Jubilee turned to mourning only eight months later, when in January 1936, King George died.

The sons of King George V – 1936-1952

King Edward VIII – 1936

1936 was a year of three kings in England. When King George V died in January, his heir became King Edward VIII. The trouble was, however, that Edward disliked his new position and thought royal ceremonial stuffy and boring. He had preferred being Prince of Wales, for then he travelled the world, met people from all walks of life and acted as a sort of royal ambassador for England.

This exciting life ended when Edward became king. To make matters worse, Edward was too liberal-minded to get on well with the Conservative government and he wanted to marry an American woman, Mrs Wallis Simpson, who would not be acceptable as queen. For Mrs Simpson was divorced and the Church of England did not approve of divorce. The King had to choose: the throne, or Mrs Simpson. Edward chose Mrs Simpson and abdicated as king on 11 December 1936.

All this came as a great shock to the people. Some people

Mrs Wallis Simpson

thought it was very romantic for a king to give up his throne for the woman he loved. Others, however, thought King Edward had deserted his duty and were very disappointed in him. So it was necessary for Edward's successor, his brother Albert, who took the name King George VI, to restore respect for the monarchy. This had to be done at a time when another war was threatening Europe, making the first years of King George's reign years of great anxiety. What was more, George VI, like his father, was trained for the Navy, not the monarchy, and he was shy by nature and suffered from a stammer.

King George VI – 1936-1952

Queen, Elizabeth, and two daughters who were known as 'the little Princesses'. The new Royal Family soon became very popular, all the more so because by means of radio broadcasts, King George could speak directly to his people. It was a regular part of Christmas, in fact, for people to gather round the radio to listen to a special message from the King.

The new king did, however, have a great sense of duty and enjoyed the help and support of a particularly charming

This link between monarchy and people became even more important during the Second World War against Germany

The King and Queen with Princess Elizabeth and Princess Margaret (right)

London was heavily bombed during the Second World War

(1939-1945). King George and his family earned great love and respect by remaining in London even when it was being heavily bombed (1940-1941). Bombs actually fell on Buckingham Palace, the King's home in London, and the King and Queen narrowly missed being killed. After heavy raids, they used to tour the bombed areas of London, comforting people whose homes had been destroyed and whose relatives had been killed. King George also visited units of the army, war factories and battlefields overseas, in North Africa and Malta. When victory was won and the war ended in 1945, huge crowds gathered outside Buckingham Palace to cheer the Royal Family.

That day, George VI, who had been almost unknown when he succeeded his brother so unexpectedly as king, was one of the most popular men in Britain.

Queen Elizabeth II – 1952

When Queen Elizabeth II came to the throne in 1952, Britain had changed enormously since her father became king as George VI fifteen years before.

The creation of the Welfare State after 1945 had helped to lessen the gap between the rich and the poor, and Britain was no longer the centre of a great empire. Although George VI had been extremely popular, the monarchy and the court was still a bit formal and remote from ordinary people. It had to be 'modernised' and the person who achieved this was Prince Philip, Duke of Edinburgh, who had married Queen Elizabeth in 1947. Under Philip's influence, their children, Charles, Andrew, Edward and Anne all went away to school instead of being educated privately at home like the Queen. The Royal Family participated more than ever in the life of the nation, and visitors to Buckingham Palace were no

The Gold State Coach, made in the 18th century, is drawn by eight grey horses

longer mainly members of the upper classes, as before. Now, they came from all walks of life and all classes. The Royal Family also became great travellers, embarking on long 'goodwill' tours of foreign countries.

The Queen and her family now work hard as 'ambassadors' for their country and act as patrons for charities and other organisations. In a world where most countries have presidents, not kings or queens, Elizabeth II is very popular and respected. This was clear in 1977 when her Silver Jubilee was celebrated

Silver State trumpet. Fanfares at coronations are sounded on these

with great enthusiasm. A thousand years ago, the Anglo-Saxons believed there was a 'magic' about monarchy. Though the monarchy in Britain has completely changed since those times, even today some of that 'magic' still remains.

The Imperial State crown was made for Queen Victoria's coronation in 1838. It is the most valuable crown in the world and is worn for the Opening of Parliament

St Edward's crown, the crown of England, was made in 1661 for the coronation of Charles II. It is used only at coronations

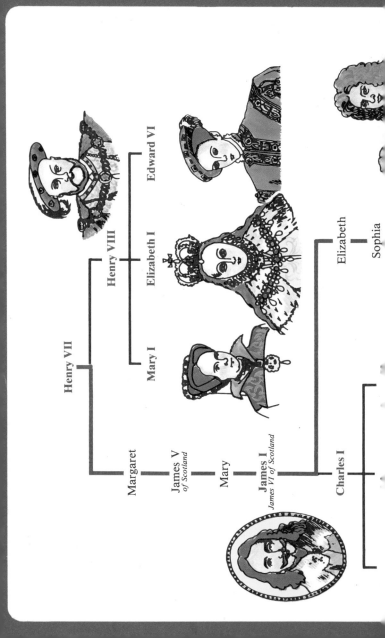

Henry VII

Margaret

Henry VIII

James V
of Scotland

Mary I   Elizabeth I   Edward VI

Mary

James I
James VI of Scotland

Elizabeth

Sophia

Charles I